D. C. [illegible]

Barnes
and the
Brains

A Creepy Case of

VAMPIRES

Other books by Kenneth Oppel

A Creepy Case of

VAMPIRES

KENNETH OPPEL

Illustrated by
Sam Sisco

Scholastic Canada Ltd.

Scholastic Canada Ltd.
175 Hillmount Rd., Markham, Ontario, Canada L6C 1Z7

Scholastic Inc.
555 Broadway, New York, NY 10012, USA

Scholastic Australia Pty Limited
PO Box 579, Gosford, NSW 2250, Australia

Scholastic New Zealand Ltd.
Private Bag 94407, Greenmount, Auckland,
New Zealand

Scholastic Ltd.
Villiers House, Clarendon Avenue, Leamington Spa,
Warwickshire CV32 5PR, UK

National Library of Canada Cataloguing in Publication Data

Oppel, Kenneth
    A creepy case of vampires

(Barnes and the brains)
ISBN 0-439-98971-X

I. Sisco, Sam. II. Title. III. Series: Oppel, Kenneth. Barnes and the brains.

PS8579.P64C74 2002   jC813'.54   C2002-900300-8
PZ7.O614Cre 2002

6 5 4 3 2 1   Printed in Canada   02 03 04 05 06

For Philippa

Contents

Chapter 1

Spooked

"YOU LOUSY GENIUSES!" shouted Mr. Wallace from his doorway, wiping water and soapsuds from his face. "That's the last time I hire you three! Pests, that's what you are! Pests!"

Giles Barnes hurried away from the house with Tina and Kevin Quark, clutching their tools, soaked to the skin.

"I think that's what you'd call an unhappy customer," Giles said.

"He sure seems upset," said Kevin.

"And why is that, do you think, Kevin?" Tina demanded angrily. "Do you think it has something to do with what happened in his kitchen just now?"

"It was an accident," muttered her brother.

"Do you think it has anything to do with the three inches of water on his floor, and the shattered dishes, and the volcano of soapsuds?"

"I told him I was sorry," Kevin mumbled.

Mr. Wallace had hired Tina and Kevin Quark's genius business to come and fix his dishwasher. It was supposed to be a simple job. But somewhere along the line, a few wires got crossed. Before anyone knew what was happening, the dishwasher had turned itself on and was spewing out water and soapsuds and dishes and glasses — and a few pots and pans, too. It was like a typhoon and a volcanic eruption rolled into one. By the time Tina had managed to shut it off, the kitchen was in ruins and Mr. Wallace was beside himself.

"You connected the wrong wires, Kevin," Tina told her brother.

"They all looked the same."

"There *were* an awful lot of wires," Giles pointed out.

"This will not be good for business," Tina said gloomily. "By the time this gets around, our brand-name credibility will be seriously damaged."

As they trudged home, wet and discouraged, none of them noticed the small, black, pointy shapes that soared overhead in the darkening sky.

* * *

"Well, Tina's banned me from the workshop," said Kevin the next day.

"Because of the dishwasher thing?" asked Giles.

"Mr. Wallace called our parents and now we have to pay him back for all the dishes we broke. Tina got really angry with me and called me a bio-hazard."

"Look, I'll chip in my share for the broken dishes. That's only fair."

Giles and Kevin were walking home past the old church at the edge of their neighbourhood. Giles had always liked the church, but not on windy evenings like this, when the trees twitched and the graveyard danced with shadows. The sun was just sinking out of sight, and fog was already rolling in off the river.

"Hey, what's that on the tower?" Kevin said suddenly.

Giles looked up at the church's bell tower. It looked like the turret of a castle, with notched crenellations and slit windows all around. Even from quite far away, Giles could clearly see that there was someone up there.

He was a tall, hunched figure, dressed in a billowing black cape. Wisps of fog curled around him, and as he turned towards them, Giles felt his knees go watery. The man's face was like a furry black mask, with only a flash of pale flesh around eyes which, in the dying light, seemed to glitter dark red.

"You see that, Barnes?" said Kevin in a quavering voice.

"I see it," whispered Giles.

The figure stretched out a bony arm, as if pointing down at them. All at once, fog boiled up around him, and when it cleared he had vanished. But swooping around the tower was a large bat, its wings slashing through the twilight.

Without warning, a whole swarm poured from the windows of the bell tower. Dozens of bats —

maybe even hundreds — wheeled through the air, flickered over the graveyard, and then swooped straight down toward Giles and Kevin.

"Run!" Giles shouted.

With their shoulders scrunched up around their ears and their hands clamped over their heads, the two boys charged past the graveyard. They didn't dare to look back. They veered around the next corner, barrelled on down the street, and didn't stop running till they'd reached Kevin's house.

Chapter 2

Wooden Stakes and Silver Bullets

"A VAMPIRE?" Tina said.

"Sure looked like it," puffed Giles, still breathless. "Tall, black cape, pale skin — the works."

"A vampire," she said again slowly, as if rolling the thought over in her head. She smiled faintly. "How interesting. How quaint."

"*Quaint*?" exclaimed Kevin. "You should have seen it!"

Tina sighed and put down the fat science textbook she'd been reading for fun. She didn't look much like her brother, who was tall and gangly, with curly red hair and freckles. Tina was quite small, with two perfect blond braids and a crease in her forehead — because she was always thinking hard about her next brilliant scientific break-through. Giles was certain she was the smallest genius in the world.

"And there were bats everywhere!" added Kevin. "That's what vampires do, isn't it? They turn into bats!"

"Kevin," sighed his sister, "I think your brain is overheated. And Barnes, you aren't much better."

"You weren't there!" Giles objected. "It was terri-fying!"

"We're going to need garlic," Kevin began, counting off on his fingers. "We're going to need holy water, we're going to need wooden stakes and silver bullets, we're going to need — "

"Vampires don't exist," said Tina calmly. "What you saw was just a regular person on the church tower — probably one of the bell ringers."

"They only come during the day!" said Giles, who could hear the church bells from his house.

"And how do you explain the bats?" Kevin demanded.

"Bats always come out at dusk," said Tina. "They are nocturnal animals. That means they feed at night."

"Feed at night," said Kevin in a strangled voice. "Did you hear that, Barnes? They're *feeding* at night. Here. In our neighbourhood!"

Giles swallowed. He didn't like the sound of that one little bit.

"All right," sighed Tina. "Tomorrow we'll go have a look at the church. But this is all very unscientific. I just want you to know that."

* * *

After school the next day, Giles, Kevin and Tina headed back to the old church. As they neared the graveyard, Kevin stopped and opened his knapsack.

"I couldn't find any garlic," he said, "but I did make a bunch of wooden stakes."

He handed Giles three short pieces of wood which had been sharpened to a point, and then plunged his hand back into his knapsack.

"I also brought a little mirror — that's how you tell if someone's a vampire, because you can't see them in a mirror. And I found an old crucifix in Mom's jewellery case. That drives off a vampire if you hold it up to his face. I called around to some stores to see if they had any silver bullets, but they said they were sold out. And anyway, they wouldn't be much use without a gun. But," he said proudly, "I did manage to get a feather duster."

He held up a ridiculous, stubby little duster with a purple handle and purple feathers.

Giles stared at it. "What's that do?" he said.

"What do you mean?" Kevin said impatiently. "It drives off vampires."

"I'm not so sure, Kevin. I've never heard that."

"Oh," said Kevin, his face falling. "I, uh, thought I heard it somewhere."

Tina sighed impatiently. "Kevin, this is all a waste of time. There's no such thing as vampires."

"I guess you don't want a wooden stake then," said Giles, offering her one.

"Please, don't insult my intelligence."

Giles and Kevin divided up the vampire gear, and Kevin reluctantly put the feather duster back in his knapsack.

"I'm sure I've heard something about feather

dusters and vampires," he muttered.

They walked through the graveyard, past crooked tombstones worn smooth by time. Giles had to admit that, in broad daylight, the church didn't look nearly as scary as it had last night. Maybe Tina was right after all. But he was still glad to have a wooden stake and mirror handy.

"You say you saw someone up there?" said Tina, pointing to the bell tower.

"Yes," said Giles. There was certainly no one there now.

"Well, let's have a look inside," said Tina.

"Inside?" said Kevin. "Maybe that's not such a good idea."

"How else can we be sure?" said Tina, striding on ahead, clearly enjoying herself. "Maybe we'll find Count Dracula's coffin up there in the tower! Wouldn't that be a treat! Then you can use your stake on him! What fun!"

"I don't think she's taking this seriously," Kevin whispered to Giles.

"She's pretty sure of herself, isn't she?" said Giles. "I bet she'd be scared if she saw a real live vampire."

"Doubt it," said Kevin. "The vampire would probably take one look at her and beg for mercy."

They reached the front of the church. Around the stone archway was a border of chiselled bird heads, their ferociously sharp beaks pointing in toward the large double doors. There was no doorknob, only a huge ring of braided iron.

Tina lifted the ring and tried to turn it, but it wouldn't budge. Giles and Kevin gave it a try together, without any luck. Then Giles noticed the huge keyhole beneath the ring. He knelt down and peered through it. It was so dark inside the church that he couldn't see much.

Then it seemed to get even darker — pitch black. All at once, the door jerked away from him and he lurched forward onto the stone floor. At his nose were two big black shoes.

"The vampire!" he heard Kevin shout.

Giles looked up in terror, and saw a man in black towering above him. He scrambled backwards so fast that he knocked Kevin and Tina down onto the grass. Then he noticed the priest's white collar.

"I'm certainly no vampire," said the priest with a

faint smile. "I'm Father Peter. May I help you?"

"Oh," said Kevin, quickly stashing the wooden stake in his knapsack. Giles slowly stood up and dusted off his jeans. Father Peter was certainly not the man they'd seen last night on the tower. For one thing, the priest wasn't nearly as tall, and he was heavier, with white hair and beard.

Tina stepped forward to take charge.

"Father Peter," she said in her most businesslike voice. "Please excuse the oafish behaviour of my associates. My name's Tina Quark. This is Kevin Quark, no relation, and Giles Barnes. You may have heard of our local genius business."

"Well, I can't say I have," said Father Peter.

Tina snapped her fingers at her brother. "Kevin, our business card."

"Oh, right," said Kevin, fumbling in his pocket. He dragged out a crumpled bit of cardboard, tried unsuccessfully to smooth it, and then offered it apologetically to Father Peter.

" 'Local geniuses,' " he read aloud. " 'Capable of just about everything.' "

"Good thing he hasn't heard about the Wallaces'

dishwasher," Kevin whispered to Giles.

"We have a very impressive success rate," Tina told the priest. "And I should tell you that I'm a genius with eleven years of experience."

"How old are you?" he asked, amazed.

"Eleven," said Tina.

"I see."

"Now, Kevin and Barnes here said they saw bats in your bell tower last night."

"I don't doubt it," said Father Peter. "I've had a terrible bat problem lately. Just the last few days, really. I don't know where they've all come from. And I certainly don't know how I'm going to get rid of them!"

"Perhaps we can be of some service, then," said Tina.

Father Peter looked at her strangely for a moment. "Well, perhaps you can. Please, come inside."

Giles had never been inside this church before. It was very old, and the stone walls seemed to slope inward slightly from the roof. There were narrow stained-glass windows, and a huge baptismal font in the central aisle, made of ancient, rough stone. It was very quiet.

"It's a real problem," Father Peter told them. "You've heard that old phrase, 'bats in the belfry'? Now I know what it means! My bell pullers refuse to go up into the tower now. They say they're getting swooped by bats. And it's not just the tower. The little fiends have got into the rafters, too."

Father Peter pointed up toward the darkness of the high-beamed ceiling. Giles shuddered to think of all the bats up there, hanging upside down by their claws, wings folded tight.

"At the evening mass you can see them fluttering around. I've had people run out in terror! And, quite frankly, the droppings are becoming a real problem. All over the pews and floor!"

"Father Peter," said Tina, "I think we can solve your bat problem. I should be able to whip something up . . . quite a simple matter really . . . yes . . . yes . . . "

And Giles could see that she was momentarily lost in thought, her small head churning with numbers and formulas and mathematical symbols.

"Yes," she said after a while, "I think I know just the thing."

"Well, I'd be most grateful," said Father Peter, surprised.

"Kevin will send you an estimate," she said.

"Yes, of course," said the priest. "Running a genius business must be expensive."

"It's the cost of the human help," said Tina seriously, looking at Kevin. "Sometimes they're more trouble than they're worth. You've got to keep an eye on them."

They said good-bye to Father Peter and made their way back through the graveyard.

"Well, another job for the genius business," said Tina happily. "Should be a snap."

Giles looked back over his shoulder at the bell tower. A few bats flickered out through the slit windows into the dimming sky. He shivered. If everything was so simple, then why had all those bats come here in the first place? And who — or what — was that mysterious figure on the tower last night?

Chapter 3

Night Visitor

SCRITCH. *Scritch, screetch. Scriiiiiiiiitchhhhh.*

Giles's eyes popped open. It was the middle of the night. A strange, scratching noise was coming from outside his window. It sounded like an old, brittle twig scraping against the glass. Probably just some of those dead ivy vines his father had forgotten to cut back in the summer. But then, through the curtains, he thought he saw a strange shadow . . .

Giles slowly slipped out of bed and padded silently across the room. His heart pounded. He reached the window, took a deep breath and threw back the curtains.

There was a flash of red light from upside-down eyes. A bat hung by its claws from the outer window frame. It had thick black fur and sharply pointed ears, and Giles could see tiny, needle teeth in its open jaws.

He was frozen in terror. With a squeak, the bat quickly dropped from the window, stretched its wings and swooped down into the fog that blanketed the road. Giles's teeth chattered furiously. Just as he was about to close the curtains and dive back into bed, he heard footsteps on the pavement.

From the fog came the man they'd seen on the bell tower! He walked straight past the front of Giles's house, his black cape flowing around him, and then disappeared once more into the night.

* * *

"Mom, do we have any garlic?" Giles asked at breakfast.

"Garlic?" said his mother, looking at him strangely. "What for?"

"Oh, just vampires," said Giles breezily.

Mr. Barnes looked up from his bowl of cereal.

"Vampires?" he said.

"Garlic's supposed to protect you from vampires."

"Will you be running into many today?" his mother inquired.

"Well, you know all those bats we saw over at the old church? I think there might be a vampire with them."

"That's ridiculous," said Mrs. Barnes. She was a professor of mathematics at the university, and she didn't like anything that couldn't be explained by long equations. It was almost impossible for her to believe in anything even slightly supernatural — even the one time her own house was filled to bursting with genuine ghost birds.

"Well, Tina agrees with you," Giles told his mother. "But I'm not so sure. Anyway, we're trying to help Father Peter get rid of his bats."

"Hmm. I hope you three aren't making a nuisance of yourselves," his mother said, frowning. "I was on the phone to Mr. Wallace for almost half an hour, trying to calm him down. I don't want an angry call from the local priest next."

Giles nodded and sighed. It seemed that every

time something went wrong with the genius business, everyone forgot all the successes they'd had, and only remembered the bad things. It wasn't much fun being thought of as a pest.

"You'd better give him some garlic," Mr. Barnes said to his wife, winking at Giles.

"Humph," said Mrs. Barnes, but she started rooting around in one of the drawers. "I think I've got a few cloves around here somewhere . . . here."

She put half a bulb of garlic on the kitchen table. Giles looked at it dubiously.

"That's it?"

"Yes, that's it."

"I was kind of hoping to make a big chain, like you see in the old movies. The kind you wear around your neck."

"Well, you'll just have to make do with that, I'm afraid."

"What makes you think there's a vampire on the loose?" his father asked.

Giles told him about the spooky man he and Kevin had seen on the church tower, and about his strange reappearance last night.

"And you think he's a vampire," said Mr. Barnes.

"I'm just keeping an open mind," said Giles.

Mr. Barnes looked at the garlic on the table. "Do you think you could spare a clove or two?"

Chapter 4

A Critical Stage

"SHE STILL WON'T LET ME into the work-shop," Kevin told Giles when he arrived at the Quarks' later that day. "She says she's at a critical stage with this bat project."

"Ah."

"She's usually at a critical stage," Kevin said with a sigh, "or at least that's what she says whenever I want to get in and help. She thinks I'm a pest, Barnes — just like Mr. Wallace said."

"Well, he called all of us pests," Giles pointed out, "even Tina."

This seemed to cheer Kevin up a bit. "Well, as

long as we're all pests, I guess it's not so bad."

"Let's go see if she'll let us in now," Giles suggested.

"OK." Kevin frowned and sniffed the air. "What's that smell?"

"Garlic," said Giles, and told Kevin about what he'd seen last night.

"This is getting pretty freaky," said Kevin. "I think we've got a vampire out there, Barnes. Um, do you think you could spare some of that . . . "

Giles dug the garlic out of his jeans pocket and broke off a few cloves for Kevin. It didn't leave a lot for him. He hoped it would be enough if he ever came face to face with the vampire.

"Thanks," said Kevin, rubbing some garlic across his neck and under his arms.

Downstairs in the basement, they knocked on the workshop door.

"Who's there?" came an impatient voice.

"It's Barnes," said Kevin, and then after a pause, "and Kevin."

There was a long silence. "You can come in — *if* you don't touch anything."

They found Tina hunched over a small piece of machinery that looked like a cross between a calculator, a beat-up alarm clock and an old transistor radio.

"I believe I've come up with the answer to Father Peter's bat problem," she said.

She tightened the last screw and turned around to face them, wiping a smudge of grease off her face.

"Bats use sound to find their way around. Very high-pitched sound. Our human ears can't pick it up. But bats send out millions of little sound pulses that bounce off whatever's in front of them."

"Like an echo!" said Kevin excitedly.

"Yes," said Tina, "though I prefer the more scientific term, echolocation."

"So what's this gizmo do?" said Giles, pointing at Tina's latest invention.

"Barnes, I'd really prefer that you didn't refer to my invention as a *gizmo*." She uttered the word as if it left a particularly revolting taste in her mouth. "A *gizmo* is something a small child might make from Christmas-tree lights and Popsicle sticks. This is an invention. This is a complex piece of electronics."

"OK," said Giles, rolling his eyes at Kevin. "How does it work?"

"Well, I won't confuse you by getting too technical," she said, "but it's supposed to scare the bats away. Allow me to demonstrate."

She handed a set of headphones to Kevin.

"Put these on," she said.

"Do I have to?" said Kevin warily.

"Yes," said Tina, "it's a scientific experiment."

"Why is it always me, though?" said Kevin. "Why don't *you* put the headphones on?"

"Someone has to operate the controls," said Tina.

Reluctantly, Kevin put the headphones over his ears while Tina plugged them into her machine. She tapped various buttons, turned a few dials and finally flicked a red switch.

All at once, Kevin jerked back and all his curly hair shot straight up from his head. His eyes and mouth formed huge circles, and he immediately scrambled to push the headphones off his ears.

Watching all this, Tina merely nodded to herself in satisfaction.

"Excellent," she said.

"What was *that*?" Kevin shouted. "That's the most horrible sound I've ever heard!"

"Precisely," said Tina. "Naturally, this won't be the same sound we play to the bats. It'll be at a much higher frequency. But the principle is identical. The noise will be so frightening to them, they'll do anything to avoid it."

"I don't blame them," said Kevin, wagging his head. "My ears are still ringing."

"So we put this giz— I mean, this electronic machine of yours, in the church," said Giles, "and it scares the bats away. Kind of like a scarecrow."

"I've decided to call it the Bat Zapper," said Tina proudly. "Now, let's go show Father Peter." She paused and sniffed the air with distaste. "Is that garlic?"

* * *

"Do we really have to go up here?" said Giles.

"Yes," said Tina. "It's essential that we put the Bat Zapper as close as possible to the bats."

Giles, Tina and Kevin, with Father Peter in tow, slowly made their way up the narrow, spiral staircase to the bell tower. Even in mid-afternoon it was quite dark, and Giles had to guide himself by trailing a hand along the cold, damp stone. He was glad Father Peter was with them. A priest could ward off vampires, couldn't he?

"Now, be very quiet," whispered Tina. "We don't want to wake up the bats."

They reached the top of the tower and padded around the big shaft where the bells hung. There were three of them, each a different shape and size, and through the hole in the floor, Giles could see straight down into the church.

"What a stink!" gasped Kevin, plugging his nose.

"Bat droppings," whispered Father Peter, pointing to the floor.

"At least there's no sign of a coffin for the you-know-what," Giles whispered to Kevin.

"Shhhh!" Tina hissed.

Pale rays of light filtered through the slit windows. As Giles stared up into the darkness, he couldn't see a thing at first, but then, as his eyes adjusted, he could make out hundreds of small black and brown shapes, roosting among the timbers and stone.

"There are zillions of them!" Kevin gasped.

Tina was already at work, setting down her machine and twiddling the dials and knobs.

"It'll turn itself on in one hour," she said to Father Peter. "And then you should be bat-free within a day."

"I hope it works," said the priest.

"Me too," Giles said, staring at the mass of bats overhead. "Let's get out of here."

Chapter 5

One More Chance

"IT'S A DISASTER!" Father Peter cried when they came back the next day. He met them in front of the church doors. "There are more bats than ever!"

"Impossible," said Tina with a frown. "The Bat Zapper is supposed to scare them off."

"Well, it's not working," said Father Peter. "It's *attracting* them!"

"I'd better take a look," said Tina.

Kevin and Giles followed her to the doors, carefully pushed them open and poked their heads inside the church. Giles couldn't believe what he saw. It sent an icy tingle through his whole body. The whole church was teeming with bats, swarming excitedly like a thick cloud of giant bees. You could barely see to the altar, the bats were so thick. The air throbbed with their chorus of high-pitched squeaks and squeals.

They stepped back outside and quickly slammed the door shut.

"I don't understand," said Tina. "All my calcula tions . . . those bats should not be here!"

"Well, they are!" shouted Father Peter. "How am I supposed to conduct mass now? My own fault for hiring three children, I suppose."

"At least he still doesn't know about the dishwasher disaster," Kevin whispered to Giles.

"I *do* know about the dishwasher disaster!" Father Peter roared. "Mr. Wallace told me all about it today! You've made a complete mess of things! You're fired!"

"Maybe I can be of some help," came a strange, squeaky voice behind them.

Giles turned and gasped. Standing among the tombstones in the misty graveyard was the mysterious man in the black cape.

"It's . . . it's . . . " stammered Kevin.

"I know," said Giles. "It's the vamp— "

"I'm Morley Fleder," said the man, walking toward them with a jerky, light-footed gait. "I'm a bat expert from the university. I've been studying these bats of yours."

"You're *studying* them?" said Giles in relief.

"We saw you that night on the tower!" said Kevin.

"Yes, I remember seeing you, too. I hope you don't mind," he said to Father Peter. "When I spotted the bats, I simply had to take a closer look, so I went up the tower by myself."

"We thought you were a vampire!" said Kevin.

Tina rolled her eyes wearily, but Professor Fleder laughed — a high squeaky laugh.

"A vampire, oh, that's funny," he said. "Oh, I'll have to tell my friends. They'll think that's wonderful!"

He was very tall and pointy, with thick curly black hair, big ears, and a bristly beard and moustache that spread out over most of his pale face.

Giles could understand how, from a distance, he'd thought the man was wearing a black mask. There wasn't much of his skin showing. Even his eyes looked black, but that was probably just the fading light. And Giles could see that he wasn't really wearing a cape, just a long, flappy, black raincoat.

"Well, since you're an expert," said Father Peter, "maybe you could tell me why all these bats came here in the first place."

"Simple," said Professor Fleder. "They need a new home. These bats used to live in a very nice, cozy cave down the river, but it just got bulldozed for a new office building. So now they're looking for a new place to roost."

Giles gasped in surprise. A small brown bat was crawling up the professor's arm onto his shoulder. "You've got one on you!" Giles said, pointing.

"Oh, him," said Professor Fleder, picking up the bat. "That's one of my bats from the lab. I take him out every once in a while for some fresh air. He's quite friendly. He likes being stroked, very gently, just like a mouse. See? But you mustn't ever handle a wild bat. They might bite."

Giles cautiously took a step closer and looked at the bat in Professor Fleder's hand. He had to admit that it did look a little like a mouse if you could picture it without wings. He was surprised at how small it was, really, once it was all folded up. They looked much bigger when they were flying — scarier, too. Tina was right all along. They were just animals, and here he'd been worrying about vampires! He felt a little ashamed of himself.

From his pocket, Professor Fleder took a little cloth bag, no bigger than a handkerchief, and slid the bat inside. Then he popped the bag back into the pocket of his pants.

"He's happy in there?" Giles asked.

"Very happy, yes. Very cozy. They like small spaces."

"Look, my church is not a zoo!" said Father Peter. "And as far as I'm concerned, these bats are pests! Am I going to have to spray?"

"Oh, no," said the professor in alarm. "That's a terrible thing to do to bats. You'll kill them."

"I'm certain my Bat Zapper only needs a few minor adjustments," said Tina firmly.

"Ha!" said the priest.

"Please, give us just a few more days," Giles said to Father Peter. "I'm sure we can figure something out by then."

"All right, all right," grumbled Father Peter. "I'll give you geniuses one more chance."

Chapter 6

In the Shop

THAT NIGHT, Giles sat cross-legged on his bed, trying to think up a solution to the bat problem.

He was sure of one thing. Tina's Bat Zapper wasn't the answer. Even if she did manage to fix it, it would only scare the bats off someplace else. And what if they weren't wanted *there* either? They'd just be driven off again and again.

To most people, the bats were simply pests. But the bats weren't pests on purpose. It wasn't their fault. They just wanted a place to sleep, like everybody else. Right now, they happened to be sleeping in Father Peter's church. It seemed cruel to drive them out, but Giles could understand the priest's point of view, too. People simply wouldn't come to church if it was full of bats.

The bats were looking for a new home. That's what the professor had said. But how did you find a new home for bats? Maybe, Giles suddenly thought, you didn't have to find one.

Maybe you could build one.

* * *

"Bat boxes?" said his father.

"That's what they're called," said Giles, showing him the plans he and Kevin had photocopied that morning at the library. "See, you nail them high up on trees, and the bats come inside through a narrow opening in the bottom and roost there. We thought we could build some for the church bats. It's only fair, after all. Their last home got bulldozed, so it's up to us to build them a new one. But we'd need your help, Dad."

"Well," said his father, leafing through the plans. "Some of these deluxe models might be a little too ambitious for beginners — like this bat mansion, for instance."

"We can leave out the fake skylight," said Kevin helpfully. "And the porch columns and bay windows."

"We want it to be nice, though," said Giles.

"They're just bats!" said Mr. Barnes. "Do they need electricity and indoor plumbing, too?"

"Well, why don't we build some of these smaller ones, then," said Giles.

"Good idea," his father agreed. "Tina won't be joining us?"

Kevin shook his head. "No. She's back home, still trying to fix the Bat Zapper. And she sure doesn't want my help."

"Still locked out of the workshop?" Giles asked.

"Yep."

"Never mind," said Mr. Barnes, rolling back his sleeves. "There'll be plenty of work to do here. Let's get started, shall we?"

In Mr. Barnes's garage workshop, they began by marking out the measurements of all the different bat box parts on the wood planks. Mr. Barnes showed Giles and Kevin how to saw in a perfect straight line, and then how to nail two pieces of wood snugly together.

"You two are catching on really fast," said Mr. Barnes. "I'm impressed."

"Thanks, Dad."

"Thanks, Mr. Barnes," said Kevin, beaming at this rare compliment.

"So, what happened to that vampire of yours?" Mr. Barnes asked.

"He wasn't a vampire after all, just a bat expert from the university."

"Oh," said Mr. Barnes, "so I guess I don't need that garlic anymore."

"No," Giles said with a grin. Not that there weren't some strange things about Professor Fleder. For a start, he really was unusually pale. But then again, Giles supposed anyone would be pale if they worked nights, studying bats. You'd hardly ever see the sun. And as for those big ears that were just a little pointy on top, and that strange, squeaky voice, and that thick, furry black beard — well, Giles told himself reasonably, that was just the way Professor Fleder was. Lots of people had funny ears and voices and beards!

"And you know what else?" said Giles. "When I

was in the library, I did some reading up on bats. They're not so scary after all. And they're not pests, really. Their droppings make excellent fertilizer, and they eat all sorts of insects, especially mosquitoes."

"Sounds good to me," said Mr. Barnes.

"And it's only vampire bats that drink blood, and they only live in tropical countries. So I guess we were pretty silly to be worrying about vampires."

"Oh, well," said Kevin, "I knew there wasn't anything to be afraid of. If you don't mind me saying so, Barnes, you always were a little on the superstitious side."

"Me?" exclaimed Giles. "What about you? With your wooden stakes and mirrors and feather dusters!"

"Oh, that," said Kevin. "I was just trying to make you feel better."

"Right!"

* * *

After a few hours, the bat boxes were beginning to look like the pictures in the plans. "This is fun," said Kevin happily. "I think I've got a knack for this."

There was a knock on the garage door.

"Hello?" Giles called out.

"Barnes, it's Tina."

Giles shot Kevin a smile. "Tina?" he said doubtfully. "Tina who?"

"Tina Qu— you know very well who it is! I just came to see what you two were working on."

"I'm afraid we're rather busy right now, Tina," said Giles.

"We're at a *critical stage*," said Kevin.

"Yes, that's right, a critical stage," said Giles. "We really can't be disturbed right now."

"Oh," came Tina's voice. She sounded a little taken aback. "I see. Well, what are you working on in there?"

"We wouldn't want to confuse you by being too technical, but we'll be glad to show you our inventions when they're all done," said Giles.

"Tell Mom and Dad I'll be home for dinner," Kevin called out.

"Well . . . all right . . . "

They waited for Tina's footsteps to die away, and then they burst into laughter.

"You were a little hard on her, weren't you?" said

Mr. Barnes, but Giles could see that he was smiling, too. "Well, maybe not," he said. "Let's get back to work. We'll be finished in no time."

Chapter 7

Home Sweet Home

WHEN TINA SAW the finished bat boxes the very next afternoon, the crease in her forehead deepened. She examined them in silence, her hands clasped studiously behind her back.

Giles and Kevin looked at each other nervously, wondering what critical thing she was going to say.

"Kevin," she said finally, "did you help make these?"

"Yes," he said. "That one over there is mine."

"I see." She fell silent for another moment, then cleared her throat and said, very quietly and quickly, "Well done."

Kevin just stared at his sister, dumbstruck.

"Did you just say, 'Well done'?"

She gave a little nod.

"You're kidding, right?"

She shook her head.

Kevin looked at Giles and smiled. "Would you mind saying that again, Tina, just so I'm sure?"

Through gritted teeth she said, "You've done good work here, Kevin." It was obviously very difficult for her to say.

"How did the Bat Zapper go?" Giles asked Tina.

"Not . . . good," she said, blushing. "I don't seem to be able to fix it at such short notice. In fact, it's a complete failure."

"Oh, I don't think so," said Giles with a smile. "I've been thinking about the Bat Zapper, and I think it'll come in handy. Could you go get it?"

"Really?" Tina asked in surprise.

After she got back, they all set off for the church-yard with the bat boxes and tool kit.

* * *

"It's handsome work, all right," said Father Peter, as he admired the sanded pine and neat joints of the bat boxes. "But how do we know the bats will move in right away?" He was beginning to sound a little grumpy again. "I can't wait any longer for them to clear out, you know."

"Well, I read up on it, and you're right," said Giles. "Normally, it could take years for bats to move into bat boxes. But I've got a plan."

"Hmm. Another plan," said Father Peter. "Well, let's give it a try. Where do we put these things?"

"What about those oak trees at the edge of the graveyard?" said Giles. "We'll need to hammer them about twenty feet up, facing south."

"I'll go get the ladder," the priest said.

"Oh, are those bat boxes?" came a squeaky voice from behind them. Giles turned with a start. It was Professor Fleder, walking toward them.

Giles and Kevin proudly showed him their boxes.

"Very nice," he said, taking one in his pale hands and peering into the slit-like opening. "Lots of rough surfaces for them to hang on, the joints are nice and snug. We like to be warm and cozy at night — I mean, the bats do. Yes, yes, very nice, very nice indeed . . ."

"He's been around bats a bit too long, if you ask me," Kevin whispered to Giles.

"A bit batty, you think?" Giles whispered back.

"Definitely," snickered Kevin.

Professor Fleder put down the bat box. He took a small box of candy from his pocket, jiggled a few into his palm and popped them quickly into his mouth. Giles only caught a quick glimpse of them, but he'd never seen such weird-looking chocolates before. One of them looked almost like a beetle!

"Care for one?" said the professor, holding out the box.

"No, no, that's all right," said Giles.

"Mmmmm," said Professor Fleder in his high squeaky voice, continuing to chomp and chew. "They're very good."

Father Peter returned with the ladder, and they set about fastening the bat boxes to the oak trees. It was tricky work, and by the time they were finished, it was starting to get dark. Finally, Giles went up the ladder one last time and hung the Bat Zapper on a nail, right beneath the opening of one of the boxes.

"Of course!" exclaimed Tina. "You're going to

use the Bat Zapper to *attract* them!"

"Good idea, Barnes," said Kevin.

Following Tina's instructions, Giles flicked the switch on the gadget, and then climbed back down.

All eyes now turned to the bell tower. For a moment, everything was very still. Then the first pair of wings emerged from a slit window and circled around and around the tower. Soon another bat appeared, then a third, and together they streaked low over the graveyard toward the oak trees, fluttering around the bat boxes.

One of the bats landed on a tree trunk, gripping the rough bark with its claws, and peered down at the bat box. The second bat landed beside the box, and the third flipped upside down and gripped hold of the tree right underneath, sniffing and squeaking at the slit-like entrance at the bottom.

"They're checking it out," Professor Fleder whispered to Giles.

"I hope it works," Giles mumbled.

With a quick upward twist, the bat underneath the box disappeared inside.

"One's gone in!" said Father Peter. "I saw it."

Giles waited anxiously for the other two bats to go in. But they remained outside. What was going on? Was something wrong? Then the other bat came out again and flew around agitatedly, squeaking to the others.

"He doesn't like it!" groaned Giles.

The three bats lit from the tree and swooped back up to the bell tower.

"Does this mean they're not moving out?" said Father Peter.

Kevin patted Giles comfortingly on the shoulder. "Maybe they just need a little longer to get used to the bat boxes," he said.

Giles felt terribly disappointed. He'd let everyone down, and now Father Peter would go back to thinking they were all pests, just like the bats. But he couldn't help noticing that Professor Fleder was smiling to himself as he stared at the bell tower.

"Well, it didn't work," said Giles. "Sorry, Father Peter."

"Wait . . . " said Professor Fleder in his squeaky voice. "Wait just a second . . . "

All at once, a huge cloud of bats burst from the tower, soaring across the graveyard toward them. Giles ducked as they streamed overhead, circling the trees. They landed all over the trunks; some right on the bat boxes themselves. Then, quickly, in twos and threes, they swooped down toward the entrances of the boxes and disappeared inside.

"It's working!" cried Giles. "They're moving in!"

"They were just waiting for the first bats to give them the OK," said Professor Fleder.

"I just hope they all fit in there," said Father Peter.

"Oh, they will," said the professor. "Bats like snuggling close together. They're very social animals. They don't need much space."

They watched in amazement as more and more bats flapped toward the trees and landed inside the bat boxes.

"Well," said Father Peter, turning to Giles and the Quarks. "I owe you three an apology. I'm sorry I lost my temper earlier. You're not pests at all. Without the genius business, I'd be shovelling bat droppings off the church floor until New Year's!"

"I owe you an apology, too, Kevin," said Tina. "I

shouldn't have locked you out of the workshop."

"Well, I did mess up the dishwasher thing," said Kevin humbly.

"Yes, you did," agreed Tina. "That was, of course, completely your fault. But then again, look at what I did with the Bat Zapper. Anyway, you're free to return to the workshop if you like."

"Really?"

"Yes."

"Can I help out with the next invention?"

"Within reason, yes," said Tina slowly.

"And can we test it on you next time, instead of me?"

"Don't push it, Kevin. This has been a hard day for me."

"Well, I've got to go and prepare for tomorrow's mass," said Father Peter happily. "I can hardly wait — a mass without bats!"

He said good-bye to all of them and carried the ladder back across the misty graveyard to the church, whistling as he went.

Professor Fleder was still gazing up at the brand-new bat boxes.

"Excellent work, you three. I'm very impressed. You should consider becoming bat experts."

"We should be getting home," said Giles, noticing how dark it had become. "Good-bye, Professor."

"Good-bye," said Professor Fleder, walking off across the graveyard with his strange, jerky gait. "And thank you very much."

"For what?" Giles asked.

"For giving us a new home," Professor Fleder replied.

Giles, Kevin and Tina looked at each other.

"Hey, what do you mean, *us*?" called out Giles.

Suddenly Professor Fleder wasn't there anymore. But from out of the mist flapped a bat, slightly larger than the others, with thick, curly black fur and pointy ears. As Giles, Tina and Kevin stood there, dumbfounded, it circled around their heads a few times, squeaking happily. Then it streaked toward one of the bat boxes, did a neat backward somersault in mid-air, and disappeared inside.

For a moment, no one said a word.

"Um, did he just turn . . . " said Giles.

"Was it just my imagination or . . . " said Kevin.

"I, ah, don't really . . . " said Tina.

They all fell silent again for a moment.

"Well, we should probably be getting back now," Giles said, starting quickly across the shadowy graveyard.

"Yeah, good idea," Kevin said, following after him.

"Hey, do you have any of that garlic left?" Tina asked, hurrying to keep up.

Kenneth Oppel's first book, *Colin's Fantastic Video Adventure,* was published when he was fifteen years old. Since then he has written many more books, including the best-selling novels *Silverwing*, *Sunwing* and *Firewing*, and won the Mr. Christie's Book Award and the Canadian Library Association's Book of the Year for Children Award.

Kenneth lives in Toronto with his wife and two children.

The first exciting
Barnes and the Brains adventure!

Giles Barnes and his family have just moved — into a very strange house. Creaks, rustles, and fluttering sounds fill his bedroom. His mother insists there is no such thing as ghosts, but Giles decides to investigate. He enlists the help of his new neighbours, "local geniuses" Tina and Kevin Quark, and their "ghostometer," and together Barnes and the Brains solve the mystery — and get rid of the ghosts for good!

A Bad Case of Ghosts
by Kenneth Oppel
ISBN 0-590-51750-3
$4.99

Barnes and the Brains, back on the case!

When Giles, Tina and Kevin see books moving in the library, all by themselves, they know they have to investigate. But Tina's amazing ghostometer doesn't pick up any ghosts, so what could that mysterious presence be? Nobody expects what they actually find — and once again, it takes a dose of Giles's own common-sense magic to get things back to normal.

A Strange Case of Magic
by Kenneth Oppel
ISBN 0-439-98732-6
$4.99

More mayhem for Barnes and the Brains!

Tina Quark has invented the ultimate robot! The
Tinatron 1000 is programmed to perform any task
flawlessly — from cleaning to homework, and everything
in between. When Tina asks Giles Barnes to robot-sit,
the robot's perfect ways drive him perfectly crazy. And
when Tinatron's circuits start to overload, sparks fly!
Can Barnes and the Brains outsmart a renegade robot?

A Crazy Case of Robots
by Kenneth Oppel
ISBN 0-439-98824-1
$4.99

Barnes and the Brains
go prehistoric!

What in the world is the strange creature floating around in the swimming pool? Barnes and the Brains have been hired to get to the bottom of the murky mystery. So they plunge in — and come face to face with not one, but two, real live dinosaurs. Soon they're hatching a plan for an amazing reptile rescue!

An Incredible Case of Dinosaurs
by Kenneth Oppel
ISBN 0-439-98792-X
$4.99

Another sticky situation
for Barnes and the Brains!

A blue glow is slowly spreading over Aunt Lillian . . .
This wrinkle cream is going too far. Giles's aunt has
become a kid again, and everybody's treating her like
one. It's time for Barnes and the Brains to outsmart the
super-goo, and get Giles's kooky Aunt Lillian back into
her own skin!

A Weird Case of Super-Goo
by Kenneth Oppel
ISBN 0-439-98793-8
$4.99